Malaika's Surprise

TEXT BY
Nadia L. Hohn

PICTURES BY
Irene Luxbacher

GROUNDWOOD BOOKS
HOUSE OF ANANSI PRESS
TORONTO / BERKELEY

Groundwood Books / House of Anansi Press
groundwoodbooks.com

Groundwood Books respectfully acknowledges that the land on which
we operate is the traditional territory of many nations, including
the Mississaugas of the Credit, the Anishnabeg, the Chippewa, the
Haudenosaunee and the Wendat peoples.

We gratefully acknowledge for their financial support of our publishing
program the Canada Council for the Arts, the Ontario Arts Council
and the Government of Canada.

Canada Council   Conseil des Arts
for the Arts   du Canada

ONTARIO ARTS COUNCIL
CONSEIL DES ARTS DE L'ONTARIO
an Ontario government agency
un organisme du gouvernement de l'Ontario

With the participation of the Government of Canada | Canada
Avec la participation du gouvernement du Canada

Library and Archives Canada Cataloguing in Publication
Title: Malaika's surprise / Nadia L. Hohn ; pictures by Irene Luxbacher.
Names: Hohn, Nadia L., author. | Luxbacher, Irene, illustrator.
Identifiers: Canadiana (print) 2020025345X | Canadiana (ebook)
20200253468 | ISBN 9781773062648 (hardcover) |
ISBN 9781773062655 (EPUB) | ISBN 9781773065151 (Kindle)
Classification: LCC PS8615.O396 M38 2021 | DDC jC813/.6—dc23

The illustrations were done in gouache, soft pastels and found papers,
and edited digitally.
Design by Michael Solomon
Printed and bound in Malaysia

MIX
Paper from
responsible sources
FSC® C012700
FSC www.fsc.org

For my real-life surprise, my baby sister
Tierra, but also in memory of Hodan
Nalayeh, who threw me a lifeline when
I needed it. — NH

Bienvenue *— Welcome

Bonne fête à toi * — Happy birthday to you

Carnaval ici * — Carnival is here

Doubles — An Indo-Trinidadian street food
made of two pieces of fried dough
filled with curried chickpeas, hot
sauce, tamarind and other chutney
toppings

Famille *— Family

Habibti ** — My love

Je sais * — I know

Notre petit frère *— Our little brother

Qui * — Who

Soca — Music that developed in the 1970s
in Trinidad and Tobago, when calypso
music was influenced by Indo-Caribbean
rhythms, R&B, soul and disco

Un petit bébé *— A little baby

Yalla ** — Let's go

*French   **Arabic

IT'S SUMMERTIME. EVERY DAY, ADÈLE and I put on masks and colorful capes to play carnival. We dance to the soca music coming from the windows of our house. We sing, "Carnival is here, *carnaval ici …*" again and again, until we fall down laughing.

I see a little girl looking at us.
"Who's that?" I say.
"Qui?" Adèle ask.
But the little girl is gone.
"Malaika, Adèle," Papa Frédéric
call. "Dinnertime."
"Okay, Papa," we say,
dragging our feet home.

At dinner, I ask Mummy, "Can the little girl next door come out to play?"
"Which little girl?" she ask me.
I tell Mummy about her.
"Sounds like a new little friend," she say.

"Not the only new little one," say Papa Frédéric.

"Girls, you will have a baby brother or sister soon."
Mummy smile, rubbing her belly. "Around the time of your
birthday, Malaika."

"Yay! *Un petit bébé*," Adèle say, clapping her hands.

"What?" I ask.

What will it be like when the baby come?
Will Mummy forget about me?
I try to finish my dinner, but I don't want any more.
I feel a little better when I think about school. I can't
wait to see my teacher, Madame Boulianne.

I wait and wait until the first day of school come.

When I see Madame Boulianne, I hug her. All the kids are here, and a new girl. It's the little girl from the window.

She come from a far place, just like me.
She talk a different talk too.
  Her name is Malayka M.
  Why is she crying?
  I tell her it will be okay.

Malayka M. is my new friend.

Madame Boulianne ask us to make
pictures of our families.
    I paint mine with everyone I love.
I even paint a bump on
Mummy's tummy.

Malayka M.'s picture of her family look perfect.
She is the best painter I ever see.

At home time, a tall brown
man come for Malayka M.
  "*Yalla*, Malayka, *habibti*,"
he say.
  "Like your name," Papa
Fred say to me.
  "Bye, Malayka!" I say.

At home, Mummy is knitting socks
for the baby.

When I put my hand on her tummy,
I feel little kicks.

Adèle want a girl baby to dress
up like a doll, but I don't know what
I want.

I wait and wait, and then it's my birthday.
I wake up to hugs and kisses from Mummy and
a peacock card that Adèle make. Papa Fred play
on the fiddle. Everyone sing, *"Bonne fête à toi."*

After, we have breakfast, and it's my favorite —
cornmeal porridge and fried plantain.

I hear a car beep outside.

"Our surprise is early," Mummy say.

"You'll love it." Adèle smile. *"Je sais."*

I hold my breath and close my eyes. Then I hear
the door.

"Grandma!" I cheer.

"Chile, you look like you see ghost," she say and give me a big hug.

"I miss you. Why did you come?" I ask.

"You think I was going to miss my two grandbabies' birthdays?" she say.

When Grandma come, she bring love
and sunshine, cards from my friends back
home and even my peacock carnival
costume.

Mummy say I am going to have my
birthday party at school too. Adèle and
I play carnival, dance and giggle, while
Grandma and Mummy make doubles
and a cake for me to share.

The next day after breakfast, I put on my peacock carnival costume. Adèle beg me to put make-up on my face, and I let her.

"I am ready," I say. "Let's go, Mummy …"

"Mummy?"

"Malaika, your mummy can't come today," Grandma say.

"But she promise! Can you come?"

"Sorry," Grandma say. "But it's time. The baby coming."

Papa Frédéric, Grandma and Mummy rush to the hospital, while Adèle and I take the big yellow bus to school.

When I get to school, my teacher and the kids sing
"Bonne fête" to me, but the doubles Grandma make are
cold, and the cake crush up in my bag.
It don't feel like my birthday.
I miss Mummy.

Malayka M. give me a surprise that she make — a special card for my birthday. The card have my brown and pink family. She even draw a baby.

"*Famille*," she say, and other words in her different talk as she point to a big red heart in the picture. She hold my hand and say, "All okay."

Papa Frédéric pick up Adèle and me from
school. We go straight to the hospital.
Papa Frédéric take us up in an elevator.
Where is Mummy?

"Mummy!" we cheer, and run to her.
"My girls." She smile.
We want to hug her, but … Mummy
is holding a blanket.

"Someone wants to meet you," Papa Frédéric say.
"Malaika … Adèle … This is Émile," Mummy say.
"*Notre petit frère.*" Adèle touch his yellow blanket.

"Galang chile, go hug up your baby brother,"
Grandma say.

I sit on the bed beside Adèle and Mummy. All
together, we hold my little brother.

I touch his soft hands.
Does he know I'm his big sister?
    I think of all the things I will teach him.
I know he will love carnival and soca.
    I kiss his little face.